The Stowaway

If you enjoyed reading this book, you might
like to try another story from the
Mammoth Read series:

The Boy Who Swallowed a Ghost
  Vivien Alcock
Name Games Theresa Breslin
Shadowflight Franzeska G Ewart
£10,000 Keith Gray
The Runner Keith Gray
Dead Trouble Keith Gray
The Gargoyle Garry Kilworth
Barney's Headcase Lynne Markham
Winter Wolf Lynne Markham
Is That Your Dog? Steve May
Little Dad Pat Moon
Ghost in the Glass Caroline Pitcher
Tommy Trouble Stephen Potts
Hurricane Summer Robert Swindells
Roger's War Robert Swindells
Doodlebug Alley Robert Swindells
Size Twelve Robert Westall

The Stowaway

William Bedford

Illustrated by

Claire Fletcher

EGMONT

For my father
i.m.
(10.12.1918 – 7.2.2001)
W.B.

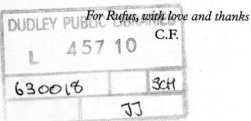

For Rufus, with love and thanks
C.F.

First published in Great Britain in 2001
by Mammoth, an imprint of Egmont Children's Books Limited
a division of Egmont Holding Limited
239 Kensington High Street, London W8 6SA

Text copyright © 2001 William Bedford
Illustrations copyright © 2001 Claire Fletcher

The moral rights of the author and illustrator have been asserted

ISBN 0 7497 4273 9

1 3 5 7 9 10 8 6 4 2

A CIP catalogue record for this book is available from the British Library.

Typeset by Dorchester Typesetting
Printed in Great Britain by Cox & Wyman Ltd, Reading, Berkshire

Contents

1.	Escape	1
2.	*Dancing Sally*	11
3.	Sunk Island	27
4.	Mollies	35
5.	Sea music	49
6.	A black mark	63
7.	Fathers and sons	73
	Vanishing Spurn: a history	80
	Glossary	87

1. Escape

The school bell was ringing as Daniel ran along the quays. Any minute now, it would be too late to get to assembly: the gates would shut and Mrs Murphy would start calling the register. Daniel wanted it to be too late, so that he wouldn't have time to change his mind. He had never done such a thing before in his life. Other children in Year Six did it all the time. But Daniel had never even thought of it. He was frightened.

He ran faster. He slipped on a lump of
seaweed, righted himself, and jumped down
to the sands. He was sweating terribly.
Glancing over his shoulder, he saw with
relief that nobody was following him.

There were five Land Rovers parked on
the sands, their trailers empty now that the
fishing boats had been launched. A group
of men stood around, smoking and
glancing up at the sky, studying the

weather and the sea. There was
an onshore breeze, so the waves
looked rough, tumbling up the sands,
but Daniel knew an onshore breeze
was safe. Out at sea, the water would be
calm. He felt a thrill of excitement. He
loved the smell of the sea.

Daniel spotted his grandfather
talking with the men, his harsh
laughter carrying on the

breeze. He had given up going to sea when Daniel was born. Nowadays he spent his hours down on the foreshore, or helping launch the boats, or welcoming them when they returned. He would be telling the other fishermen stories about the old days, when he had been a fisherman like them. Daniel could not see his father among the fishermen.

He ran behind the Land Rovers and climbed up on to the groyne, where five fishing vessels were moored. The tide was high. Little waves surged against the groyne and splashed through the wooden slats, making them slippery. Daniel moved more carefully. He knew these groynes. He knew the sounds of the sea and the beach, the wonderful smells of the little fishing boats. Now that he had come this far, he was anxious to do nothing to mess up his plans.

Dancing Sally was at the far end of the
groyne, bobbing up and down with the
wash of the tide. A herring gull sat on the
tiller in the stern, staring at Daniel as he
approached. She had soft grey plumage
with black wing-tips and pink legs, and her
yellow bill had a red spot that shone when
she lifted her head warily at Daniel.

'You aren't guarding *Dancing Sally*, are you?' Daniel asked the herring gull. She flapped her wings and stabbed her beak in the air, as if she was trying to stop him boarding the vessel. Daniel looked over his shoulder quickly, then glared at the gull, darting towards her, and she flew away haughtily, screeching along the tideline. 'That'll teach you,' he said with a nervous laugh.

Daniel clambered down over the gunwales and dropped on to his knees. The school bell had stopped ringing. The teacher would be taking the register right now. Even if he ran, he would be too late for assembly. What had he done! He felt his heart racing. The air was full of the sounds of seagulls and the sea crashing up the shingle. He could still hear the voices of men, talking at the tideline.

He took a deep breath, glanced one last time over the gunwales to the fishermen down the beach, and then scrambled underneath the tarpaulin in the stern of the fishing boat.

There was no turning back now.

The Dancing Sally

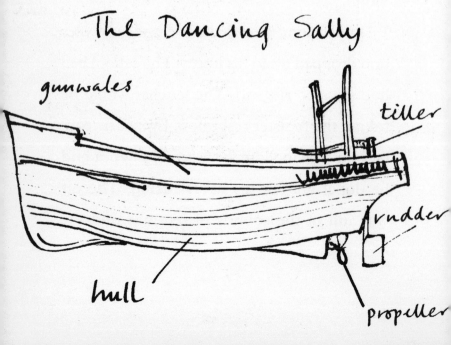

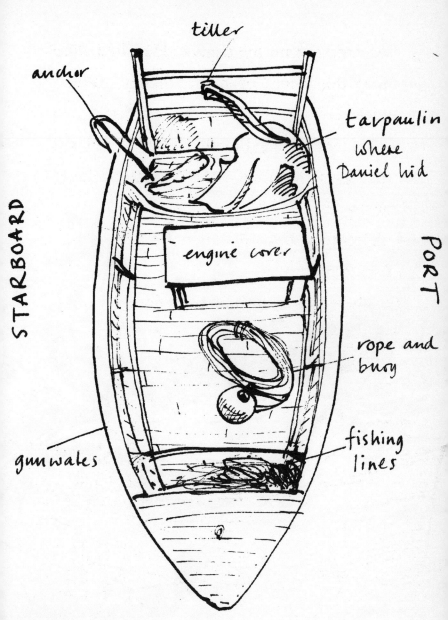

STERN

tiller

anchor

tarpaulin
where
Daniel hid

STARBOARD

PORT

engine cover

rope and
buoy

gunwales

fishing
lines

PROW

2. Dancing Sally

The roll of *Dancing Sally* as she surged away from the groynes nearly left Daniel's stomach trembling back on the shore. It was hot underneath the tarpaulin. The baited lines were coiled in a heap ready for use, and the smell of diesel was strong in the darkness. For a horrible moment Daniel wondered whether he was going to be seasick.

But he had grown up with the sea. It had been two years since his father last took him

out, but he was back where he belonged
now. He soon began to enjoy the lifting,
riding movement of the little boat. He
listened excitedly to the throb of
the outboard motor, the cry of
the gulls, the skipper whistling
and going about his work as
they buffeted through the
green water.

He knew where they were
going. They were heading
straight across the estuary to
the distant headland, a full
six miles of green water.
They were going to the spit of
land known as Spurn, where
the black and white lighthouse

perched on the edge of the sea. Off Spurn, there was a fishing ground Daniel had never visited. Very few fishermen did visit it. The very thought made Daniel shiver and go cold. He wondered how long it would take *Dancing Sally* to get there.

the lighthouse at Spurn

By the time the engine was at last turned off, and Daniel heard the anchor rattling down into the sea, he was tense with excitement.

This was the moment he had been dreading.

Abruptly, the skipper lifted the tarpaulin back to get at his baited fishing lines.

Brilliant sunshine blazed down from the sky.

'Daniel!' the skipper gasped. 'What the devil!'

'Dad!'

Daniel blinked the sun out of his eyes and

pushed the tarpaulin aside. He scrambled to his feet, slipping against the pile of baited lines, gulping the fresh air into his lungs. Nervously, he stared at the skipper, trying to read the expression on his face.

His father was a moody man. He sometimes lost his temper, and then his voice was as big as the January tides, surging and crashing up the foreshore of your ears. When he was calm, his voice was musical and he sang songs. Sometimes, when Daniel was in bed at night, he heard his father singing to himself in the kitchen or the small backyard, playing his melodion.

'Did you want these, Dad?' Daniel said at last, taking a deep breath and handing him the snoods baited with fat lugworms.

His father was staring down at him, frowning and scratching his head, his blue eyes shining with the light from the sea.

lugworm

'You can put those down,' he said tersely. 'What in the name of all that's wet do you suppose you're doing here? You're supposed to be at school.'

'I know, Dad . . .'

'Then what are you doing here? There's nowt wrong at school, is there?' he asked suddenly, looking worried.

'No, Dad.'

'Then we're going straight back to shore, you're going . . .'

'Let me help, Dad. I can help.'

'I don't need help!'

'I always used to help you!' Daniel cried, the hurt welling up inside him, his eyes beginning to itch with tears. 'I used to help you when Mum was alive!'

His father looked astonished, caught off guard, his eyes sharp and considering.

A flock of herring gulls suddenly appeared out of the sky, following the wake of the *Dancing Sally*. They wheeled and squawked around the idling vessel.

Daniel's father glanced up into the sky, and shook his head slowly. 'Too late to go

back now,' he said. 'And the gulls have seen the lugworms. We'd better get the lines over the side.'

'I can do that, Dad,' Daniel said quickly, his voice trembling with excitement.

His father glanced at him again, about to say something, then ruffled his hair instead. 'You'd better call me skipper if we're on a trip,' he said, his voice still rough but his eyes laughing. 'Like you've joined the crew.

And if you're on my boat, you have to work.'

'Yes, Skipper.'

For several minutes neither of them spoke as they got the lines over the starboard side. The long-lines disappeared into the dark waters of the sea, while the herring gulls screamed up above, diving and wheeling in the sunlight, trying to get the bait before it

sank beneath the surface. A cormorant
sailed to their starboard and landed
on one of the groynes near the
lighthouse on Spurn.

cormorant

Daniel concentrated on the work. This
was what he had been hoping for. There
was nothing like fishing, especially
alongside his dad. But his dad had kept on
promising and then finding an excuse,
postponing the trip, saying it was the

weather, or there were no fish, or telling Daniel to get on with his work at school. There was always some good reason why Daniel couldn't go out in *Dancing Sally*.

His father still took him bait-digging some mornings, long before school. It was a rare world, getting up at five o'clock on a freezing winter morning. Waders would be swarming along the sands. Godwits and curlews were the ones that took the best lugworms, their long beaks digging down into the sands, their hungry cries haunting the dawn silence.

bar-tailed godwits

Daniel loved it. Looking up, you would see a thin line of light over the horizon, a trawler maybe heading down the river for the estuary. High in the dark sky, a tern would suddenly begin its call, a restless *tirrick* echoing along the shores. Once the herring gulls began their screaming noise, you wouldn't be able to hear anything else at all.

Going bait-digging was great, but it still wasn't like being out at sea in a small boat, trying to catch fish. That was what Daniel had been missing: the sea, and having Dad all to himself.

tern

herring gull

When they were done
with the lines, Daniel's
father sat down in the stern and
lit his pipe. Daniel waited for him
to say something, to give Daniel a
chance to explain.

'What's this all about then?'
his father said with an ironic smile. 'You
reckon on giving up school?'

Relief flooded over Daniel like the tide.
His father wasn't angry. He wasn't going to
get into one of his stormy moods.

'Sorry, Dad.'

'It's all right by me. I never reckoned
much to school. Your mum wouldn't be too

pleased though, if she were here. She thought your lessons were important.'

'I can catch up on my lessons, Dad.'

'I know you can. But that ent the point, far as I can see. When you're supposed to be in a place, you're supposed to be there.'

'Yes, Dad,' Daniel said warily, wondering whether his father's sympathy was slipping away.

'You know that's what your mum wanted.'

'Yes,' he replied quietly.

Daniel was eleven. His mother had died two years ago, and he could still remember her smell: of the sea, and lavender, and seashells. She lived all her life by the sea in their town. She had even fished with Dad before Daniel was born; *Dancing Sally* was named for her, to bring them good fortune, and she always had. She said *Dancing Sally* came from the sea, like a mermaid.

Daniel felt the tears pricking. He didn't want to talk about his mum. He didn't want to think about her. Not now. 'This isn't about Mum,' he said quickly.

His father glowered, his suntanned face like old mahogany. 'Then you'd better explain yourself, lad,' he said sternly.

Daniel looked straight at his father.

'I miss going out with you, Dad. I heard you and Grandad talking last night, about Sunk Island. I ent never been to Sunk Island. I want to go with you.'

3. Sunk Island

It had been dark when the two men took their beers out into the backyard and started talking about Spurn.

'You got to be joking!' Daniel's grandad had said with a loud snort of surprise. 'It's too dangerous.'

'I ent joking,' Daniel's father said seriously.

'Then you're losing it, son, you're going off the end of the pier. That's what I reckon.

Nobody fishes Sunk Island. Nobody in their right way of thinking.'

There was a long silence. Daniel was crouching at the top of the stairs in the darkness. He had spent the evening helping his dad bait the snoods ready for fishing, and then gone to bed. His grandad came home late, and the two men sat in the small backyard, each with a bottle of beer and talking like they always talked, about the next day's fishing.

And Daniel knew why his grandfather was so surprised. A shiver ran down his spine when he heard mention of Sunk Island, the fishing-ground just off Spurn the far side of the estuary.

'There's drowned fishermen off Sunk

Island,' his grandad's voice said solemnly in the dark yard.

'There's drowned fishermen all over the sea,' Daniel's father grunted in reply.

'And drowned churches too!' the older man said in a strange kind of voice, like somebody preaching in a church, warning of dreadful revelations. 'Drowned churches and the ringing of drowned bells.'

Daniel's father laughed. 'I ent never heard them,' he said bluntly. 'And I don't reckon the fish will be that bothered by a few church bells. You want a cup of coffee to go with that beer you've been guzzling?'

Daniel didn't hear what his grandfather said in reply. He fled to his bed and lay in the darkness, shivering. He had heard awful stories about Sunk Island. One of their teachers had told them all about it, and the fishermen often told their own stories when they were waiting for the tides.

Centuries ago, there had been villages and a port out on Spurn. The villages were called strange names, Tharlesthorpe, Frismersk and Orwithfleet. There had been a hermitage at the end of Spurn, and the fishing port Ravenser Odd.

Ravenser Odd and all the villages had been swept away by the sea. The churches lost beneath the sea had spires which sometimes stuck up through the waves. On certain nights, you could hear the church bells ringing, and the groans of the drowned fishermen who haunted Sunk Island. If you weren't careful, you could wreck your boat on the spires of the church.

Since he first heard the stories, the voices of the drowned had cried through Daniel's dreams at night like the wailing of lonely sea birds high above the shore.

Now, Daniel took a deep breath. He spoke in a great rush. 'I'm sorry, Dad,' he said. 'I knew you wouldn't take me with you. Not to Sunk Island. But I didn't want you to go alone. I was afraid . . .'

'What you talking about, lad!'

'I was afraid. I knew you wouldn't want me to go!'

His father blinked at him thoughtfully. 'It *is* dangerous,' he said. 'But not because of daft stories about ghosts. All fishing is dangerous. That don't mean you can't go. You just go at the right time. There's a right time for things, Daniel, and a wrong. Like now is a time when you should be doing your schoolwork. Not running away to be with me.'

'But the churches were drowned!' Daniel cried. 'Mrs Murphy told us. She said it was dangerous. What if something happens to you?' Daniel's voice dropped. 'I just want to go fishing with you, Dad. That's all you've ever wanted to do, Mum told me. She said you were like that when you were at school, and I want to do it too. I want you to teach me like you used to.'

Then there were real tears in his eyes, and his father was looking at him in amazement.

4. Mossies

It took Daniel's father several minutes to check the lines and add some extra bait, and by the time he was finished, Daniel had dried his eyes. He was wondering what his father would say to his sudden outburst. When the lines were all ready, his father settled down in the stern and smiled at Daniel.

'If you are ever going to be a fisherman,' he said, 'I reckon there are some things I better tell you.'

Daniel was too surprised to speak. He didn't want to interrupt.

His father thought for a moment and then rubbed his nose. 'I'm not much good with words,' he said. 'But I reckon there's nothing frightening out here that a man can't handle: the tides, the sandbanks. You got to watch for those. You learn to know what you're doing, and then you're just careful. That's all there is to being a good fisherman.'

'But the other fishermen won't work Sunk Island,' Daniel pointed out.

'That's true,' his father nodded ruefully.

'They don't have my skills. And they're a superstitious lot, fishermen. Always ready to believe nonsense.'

A huge herring gull landed on the bows of *Dancing Sally* and Daniel's father handed him a fat lugworm to give to her to keep her away from the lines. Daniel tossed the worm high in the air, and the herring gull took off, caught the lugworm, and flew up into the wind, hanging effortlessly in the current of air while she swallowed the worm.

'They're strong birds, herring gulls,' Daniel's father said, watching the bird with admiration. 'Glide in the teeth of the wind for hours. She'll dive any minute, you see.'

Daniel watched.

The gull hovered for a long time, and then suddenly up-ended and was diving straight down at the water as if she intended finding the bottom of the sea. There was a splash, a moment of silence, and suddenly she was up again, with a codling glinting silver in her beak and squirming to be free of the air which was death to fish.

The herring gull circled *Dancing Sally* once, then swooped down again, and dropped the codling carefully into the stern.

Then she flew away screeching into the sunlight.

'Fish about then,' Daniel's father grinned.

'How'd you know, Dad?'

'She just told us, didn't she!'

They unpacked the homemade food his father had brought. They tested the lines, then ate sandwiches with apples and mugs of tea. There was more than enough for them to share. There were even chocolate bars, just in case they were out a long time and needed energy.

'You make good sandwiches, Dad,' Daniel said as he munched through his favourite, Cheshire cheese and honey pickle.

'You need to keep your strength up out here,' his dad nodded. 'But you know where the best meals are?'

'No,' Daniel shook his head eagerly, enjoying listening to his father talk.

'On the deep-water trawlers,' he said. 'The fishermen on the trawlers get the best food in the world, I reckon. Fresh cod and

haddock caught from the sea, with new potatoes and heaps of mushy peas.'

'What about pudding?' Daniel asked excitedly, his eyes shining.

His father laughed. 'You're a greedy young 'un. For pudding, my favourite was always baked syrup roll and steamed jam pudding. I love a good baked syrup roll, I do.'

One of the lines tightened against the run of the tide, and Daniel was the first to spot it. 'Well done,' his father said, and held the line gently, staring up into the sunlight, listening to the waves. The sea was dark this close to the shore, and Daniel could see a man watching them from the lighthouse at the end of Spurn. There were several dangerous sandbanks off Spurn: Greedy

Gut, Sunk Island and Old Den. He felt cold when he thought about the drowned fishermen lying below in the darkness, waltzing to the movement of the water across the white sands.

There were hundreds of seagulls swarming around Spurn now. 'They know the tides,' Daniel's father explained. 'They start gathering when the sandbanks are going to be exposed by the retreating sea, so that they can feast on the lugworms.'

There were waders already swarming along the shores, stabbing at the muddy

waders

sand. Another herring gull
landed on *Dancing Sally*'s
bows, but took off straight
away, as if surprised to see

somebody strange fishing with the skipper.

'She don't know you,' Daniel's father said
with a loud laugh, explaining the gull's rude
manners.

'I don't know her either,' Daniel said
indignantly.

'You might,' Daniel's father said with a
strange smile, puffing at his pipe.

'What do you mean?' Daniel asked.

His father was silent for a long time,
watching the white caps of the waves, the
surging of the tide.

'You won't ever be alone at sea, Daniel,'

he said at last. 'Not when the Mollies are about. Drowned friends come back as Mollies. You mustn't ever hurt them, in case they're one of your old mates, somebody you've known. You can recognise them from the way they argue: creating a fuss, making a racket, stalking up and down the deck. Your grandad reckons he knows several old fishermen who come and sit on his window ledge to tell him yarns.'

'There was a herring gull guarding *Dancing Sally* this morning. Was it a drowned fisherman?' Daniel said.

'She make a fuss when you climbed on board?'

'Yes!' Daniel said with surprise. 'Does she belong to *Dancing Sally*?'

'She might,' his father grinned. 'You never know.'

'And the one who brought us the codling this morning?'

'Another fisherman,' his father nodded solemnly.

Daniel burst out laughing. 'That's a good story, Dad,' he said, finishing his apple and throwing the core up into the air for a massive gull. 'Just the sort Grandad tells. You don't believe it really, do you?'

'No!' his father said with a laugh. Then, after another of his long pauses, 'But I wouldn't harm a Molly,' he said. 'Or paint my doors green, or sail with silver in my pockets, or leave port on a Monday morning in case I got washed away with the washing, or talk to a priest or a black cat on my way down to *Dancing Sally*. I don't believe those things at all, but I wouldn't do them, because you never know.'

Daniel was silent for a long time. These were all things he had heard his grandfather talking about at different times. His grandad was full of superstitions, things you shouldn't do. And things you *should* do, to bring good luck, like cast your nets the same side as the Lord, and throw a penny over the starboard side to buy the fish.

But Daniel had never heard his father say these things before. He usually laughed when Grandad was telling the old stories.

'Superstitions!' Daniel said, laughing now, enjoying sharing the stories with his father, being alone with him 'on the fishing' which they both loved so much.

'That's right, boy,' his father said quietly, suddenly becoming serious. 'Like I told you, you're never alone when you're at sea. You don't want to be offending the seafolk, do you?'

This time Daniel's father didn't laugh.

Daniel fell silent.

Up above them, a herring gull squawked angrily.

5. Sea music

The lines were heavy by the time the afternoon sun had climbed to the top of the sky and begun her fall back down into the sea.

Daniel's father gutted the fish rapidly, his gutting knife glinting in the light of the sun. 'It's a good catch for once,' he told Daniel cheerfully. 'Plenty of cod and codling, a few flatties. I told you Sunk Island was safe, long as you respect the sea and know what you're doing. You needn't have worried and stowed away. We'll get a good price for this lot.'

49

'I brought us luck,' Daniel said proudly.

'You did that. But times are hard, Daniel. No mistaking that. A man has to think what he's going to do.'

'I'm going to be a fisherman, like you.'

'Is that a fact?' his father said, looking surprised. 'I didn't know you'd made your mind up.'

'I want to be like you,' Daniel said, feeling proud.

'As long as there's fish,' his father said.

'There's fish in the creeks,' Daniel said. 'Grandad showed me. If I can't fish the sea, I'll fish the creeks.'

His grandfather sometimes took him fishing down the coast. Butt-pricking he called it. You fastened a barb to a shaft of

dab

wood, waded out into the shallow creeks, and thrust the barb into the water.

'Flatfish like the creeks,' Daniel told his father, as if he knew nothing about it. 'They can hide in the shallow water because it's muddy.'

He saw his father was laughing at him. 'Dabs and flounders don't make much of a supper,' he said cheerfully.

Daniel remembered the first time he'd gone with his grandfather. The old man had shown him how to use the barb.

flounder

They caught a plaice and fried it over an open fire. They had fresh bread and butter with it. His grandfather gutted and filleted the fish with a bone-handled knife he carried in his pocket.

'Not so many fish left in the creeks these days,' Daniel's father muttered now, cleaning the fish they had hauled.

'I can catch eels!' Daniel said defiantly. 'Eely Jack Bodsworth lives off the eels. He catches them in the fishdocks. I've seen him. He uses a pole with nails hammered in and drags it behind his rowing boat. The eels get caught on the nails. He sells them on the market.'

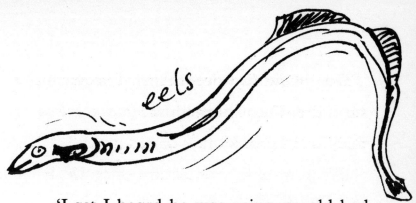

eels

'Last I heard he was using an old bed mattress,' Daniel's father said with a laugh. 'They reckon he dropped it overboard and dragged it along the bottom to catch the feeding eels. That must have been the rarest sight, all them eels falling out of that old mattress when he lifted her out of the water.'

There was an awkward pause.

'But that's not fishing,' Daniel said quietly.

'No, that's not fishing, Daniel. Out here's fishing. The sea, and the *Dancing Sally*. The magic. That's what brings me.'

Daniel's father was speaking very quietly, staring down at his hands. His voice was thick, as if he had a bad cold.

'Why wouldn't you take me, Dad?' Daniel asked.

His father shrugged. 'You're here, ent you?'

'Not since Mum died.'

His father looked up then. He was frowning, as if he didn't know what to say. There were tears in his eyes. He shook his head briefly, and Daniel thought he still wasn't going to answer, but then he put his arm round Daniel's shoulder and held him close.

'I didn't want to lose you too, boy,' he said. 'I didn't want to do that.'

Daniel felt the tears in his own eyes. 'Mum would have wanted us to be together,' he said. 'And you're a good fisherman, Dad. You know how to be careful.'

'I do that.'

'So you could teach me how to keep safe.'

'I could, aye,' his father said quietly.

They sat together for a long time, and then Daniel pulled free and grinned at his father.

'I like fishing,' he said. 'It's magic.'

'It is!' his father laughed, his voice big and booming again. 'It is magic. Eels is magic too. Did you know that, Daniel? That's why Eely Jack's lived so long. You save the life of an eel and the sea will never swallow you. That's what the old folk believe. And eels bring silver on a full moon. You stay awake and see a tide full of eels in the light of the full moon, and you'll never be short of money.'

'Is that true, Dad?'

'I don't know,' said his father. 'I ent never seen a tide full of eels in the light of the full moon. You better ask Eely Jack if you want an answer to that.'

There didn't seem to be anything else to say. Daniel yawned and suddenly felt tired. His lips tasted of salt, and his skin felt tight on his cheeks. He closed his eyes and felt the sun on his face.

Daniel's father hauled the last of the lines, gutted the fish, and fastened the tackle down. The afternoon sun was slipping down to the west now. Birds wheeled and cried along the shore on Spurn. Big vessels waited at the estuary for a pilot to take them up to the docks.

vessels waiting at the estuary

'We ready then?' Daniel's father said.

'I suppose.'

'Let's get this lot landed.'

He started the motor and *Dancing Sally* responded to the estuary tides, surging through the rough water, proudly tossing her bows. Daniel felt the salt spray on his face, the sun dazzling off the water into his eyes.

There was a sudden squawking overhead. A herring gull swooped across the stern of the vessel, wheeled away, and then came back again. She seemed to be holding something in her mouth.

On her third sweep across the wake of the fishing boat, the gull came very low and dropped something on the tarpaulin near Daniel's feet.

He bent down and looked.

It was a shell. A beautiful great scallop, with rays of red sunlight and a yellow point and delicate colouring behind the red. When Daniel picked it up it felt cold from the sea, making him shiver. He held it up to his ear. The sound of the sea sang out, but seemed to be coming from far away.

'It's a gift,' Daniel's father smiled.

'I can hear the sea,' Daniel said.

'That's right.'

'How does the sound get inside the shell?'

'It's sea music,' his father said. 'The mermaids put the music inside the shells.'

'Yes, Dad,' Daniel said, a little sceptically.

'Your mother collected seashells all the time. She reckoned sea music was the most beautiful music you could hear.'

Daniel smiled, thinking about the collection of seashells on the kitchen windowsill. His father washed them in cold water every now and then, to keep them fresh and clean. They were on a tray of seaweed Grandad picked up along the foreshore.

'Why do the mermaids put music inside the seashells?'

'It's not music, really. Not to the mermaids. More like messages. They send messages in the seashells. Like we send letters and e-mails. Only we can't understand the mermaid messages. It just sounds like the sea to us.'

'You're worse than Grandad,' Daniel said happily, and beamed into the face of the sun and tide.

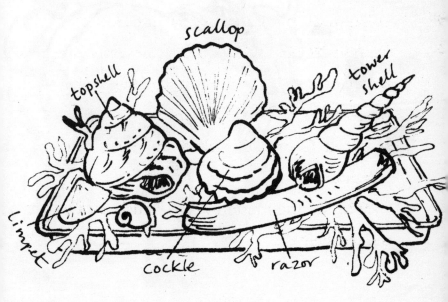

6. A black mark

The rest of the small fleet of fishing vessels had already landed their catch when *Dancing Sally* moored at the groyne. Daniel's grandfather was waiting with the trailer and Land Rover, and one of the fish merchants was there with his pony and trap.

'A good haul!' Daniel's grandfather shouted when he peered into *Dancing Sally*.

'That's a real fisherman's haul that is. And a boy as well!' he added drily. 'You catch him on your lines?'

'Summat like that,' Daniel's father laughed.

But Grandad wasn't laughing. 'Your teacher know about you bunking off, Daniel?' he asked sternly. 'She know about you going fishing?'

Daniel blushed, but his dad was in a hurry to unload the catch. 'Daniel fetched us luck,' he said, clambering out of the boat into the surging waves around the groyne. 'The best catch I've had for weeks. Now let's get this fish unloaded and find ourselves a bite to eat.'

They unloaded the catch into baskets
and put the baskets in the back of the Land
Rover. A couple of the fishermen came and
helped haul *Dancing Sally* on to the trailer.
The fishing boats were all kept in boatsheds
overnight to protect them from rough seas.

'That's a good job done,' Daniel's father told the men when *Dancing Sally* was secured. 'Thanks for the hand.'

'Goodnight then,' the men shouted, driving off with the catch.

The fish would go straight to the market for filleting ready for the dawn auction. The day's work was done.

'Have I got to go home now, Dad?' Daniel asked, crossing his fingers hard and hoping the answer would be no.

But it was his grandad who spoke first.

'Don't reckon he deserves his supper,' he said. 'Acting reckless like that. You don't play reckless with the sea. He'd be better off going and asking his mates what homework he's missed.'

Daniel's heart sank. He knew he shouldn't have hidden away on *Dancing Sally*. He should have spoken to his dad at home. His dad would be angry now. He *looked* angry, frowning irritably.

But his dad was talking to Grandad. 'Maybe he wouldn't have stowed away if I'd paid more attention, like,' he muttered, looking absent-mindedly at Daniel. 'I reckon he won't do it again.'

'Does that mean I got to go home, Dad?' Daniel asked breathlessly.

'Course not!' his father laughed. 'You've earned your supper like a regular fisherman.' Then he saw Grandad's expression. 'Don't worry, I'll have a word with Mrs Murphy. There'll be no more skiving, and he'll make up the work.'

They walked along the promenade to Brown's café and sat at one of the window tables. They could see the waves thundering up the shore in the gathering twilight. Daniel's grandfather and an old friend were talking about the fish. His father sat and drank a mug of hot sweet tea, and Daniel had lemonade with a tangy slice of lemon in it. The woman behind the counter brought through an enormous fish pie with thick slabs of haddock and shrimps and a

white sauce and mountains of mashed
potatoes. The flaky pastry melted in
Daniel's mouth.

'He's going to make a fisherman then?' Daniel's grandfather asked as they munched through the fish pie.

'I reckon,' Daniel's father smiled.

It was the best thing anybody had ever said to Daniel. He blinked hard to hold his tears back and took a long swallow of his lemonade.

'Long as Mrs Murphy doesn't give him the edge of her tongue,' his grandfather added with a wink. 'Allus good at bawling you out, schoolteachers. In my day, you'd have got your hide tanned for bunking off.'

'How'd you know that, Billy?' the other fisherman said with a grin. 'You never went to school, according to what you says.'

'I never had any shoes!' Daniel's

grandfather protested loudly. 'I couldn't walk to school without shoes. Daniel's got shoes, haven't you, boy? You can walk to school in the morning and find out what that Mrs Murphy has in store for you.'

The older fishermen laughed happily, winking and having their fun, but Daniel went cold at the thought. Mrs Murphy had a rare old temper. Even if she didn't use the cane, her tongue was nearly as bad. But that was school. He would worry about school tomorrow.

7. Fathers and sons

They walked home along the promenade. Daniel felt tired and happy after his day in the fresh air, and very full after the grand meal.

Opposite Wonderland there was a petrified forest buried deep beneath the sands, and just beyond that some of the best lugworm beds on the east coast. Daniel's grandfather knew every kind of lugworm there was, and the kind of sand they did best in.

73

cockle bed

clams

lobster

Grandad's family had worked the cockle beds for two hundred and fifty years, raking the dangerous sands and creeks, using a horse and cart to get the cockles back home for boiling. When they weren't cockling, they went push-netting along the tideline for shrimps. There were brown and pink shrimps. They also went working for crabs and lobsters, and whelks for bait.

According to Grandad, they did a bit of smuggling when times were hard.

'Sleep time, I reckon,' Daniel's father said quietly when they reached the small house overlooking the sea.

'Night, Grandad,' Daniel said sleepily.

'Night, Daniel,' he heard his grandad saying.

In bed, he snuggled down into the warmth and heard his father open the window. He liked hearing the sea as he fell asleep.

'I brought us luck, didn't I, Dad?' Daniel muttered drowsily.

'You did that,' his father said.

Crab

'You think Mum would have been proud of me?'

'When she got over being mad about school,' his father whispered. 'She'd a' been proud of you then. She always was.'

'I work at school, Dad.'

'I know you do. And I'm proud of you. You don't want to be a numbskull like me. You want to do well. I never learned a thing.'

'I want to do things, not just for Mum. Or you. I like school. But I like the fishing as well. I want to do both. Now I can. I know about it now, don't I?'

'You're a real fisherman now, Daniel.'

'Mum wanted that as well. She wanted you to be a fisherman. She loved *Dancing Sally*.'

whelk

'She did too,' his father said quietly.

'She loved the fishing.'

'She did.'

'So can I go again?'

There were tears in his father's eyes as he spoke, and his voice was gruff.

'You can, long as you do the thing properly. Long as I know. No more bunking off from school. No more leaving other work just because you feel like a trip to sea. You ask me, and we can go fishing together. I reckon your mum would have liked that. You can be my regular crew.'

Daniel drifted out to sleep then, with the great scallop shell buried under his pillow. He wanted to keep it safe. It was a present from the Molly.

In the middle of the night, he thought he woke up and heard the sea singing inside his room, but he knew that was just the messages the mermaids were sending to each other.

Then he heard the scratchy cry of a herring gull, and he knew he was dreaming about *Dancing Sally*, and the seagull that had brought him the present of the shell.

But when he opened his eyes, the Molly was sitting on his windowledge, waiting in the brilliant moonlight. Daniel sat up and tried to reach out, and the Molly lowered her beak and let him touch her gently on her silver-grey feathers. Then he went back to sleep. He knew the Molly was his own seagull, the seagull who looked after

Dancing Sally. He knew she had come back to keep an eye on him. She would always be there, as long as he needed her, as long as he lived by the sea.

Vanishing Spurn: a history

SUNK ISLAND SANDS

The east coast of England has been under attack from the North Sea for centuries. At Spurn, this attack has repeatedly destroyed and reformed the narrow spit of land, until today it is one of the strangest places in the country.

CLEETHORPES

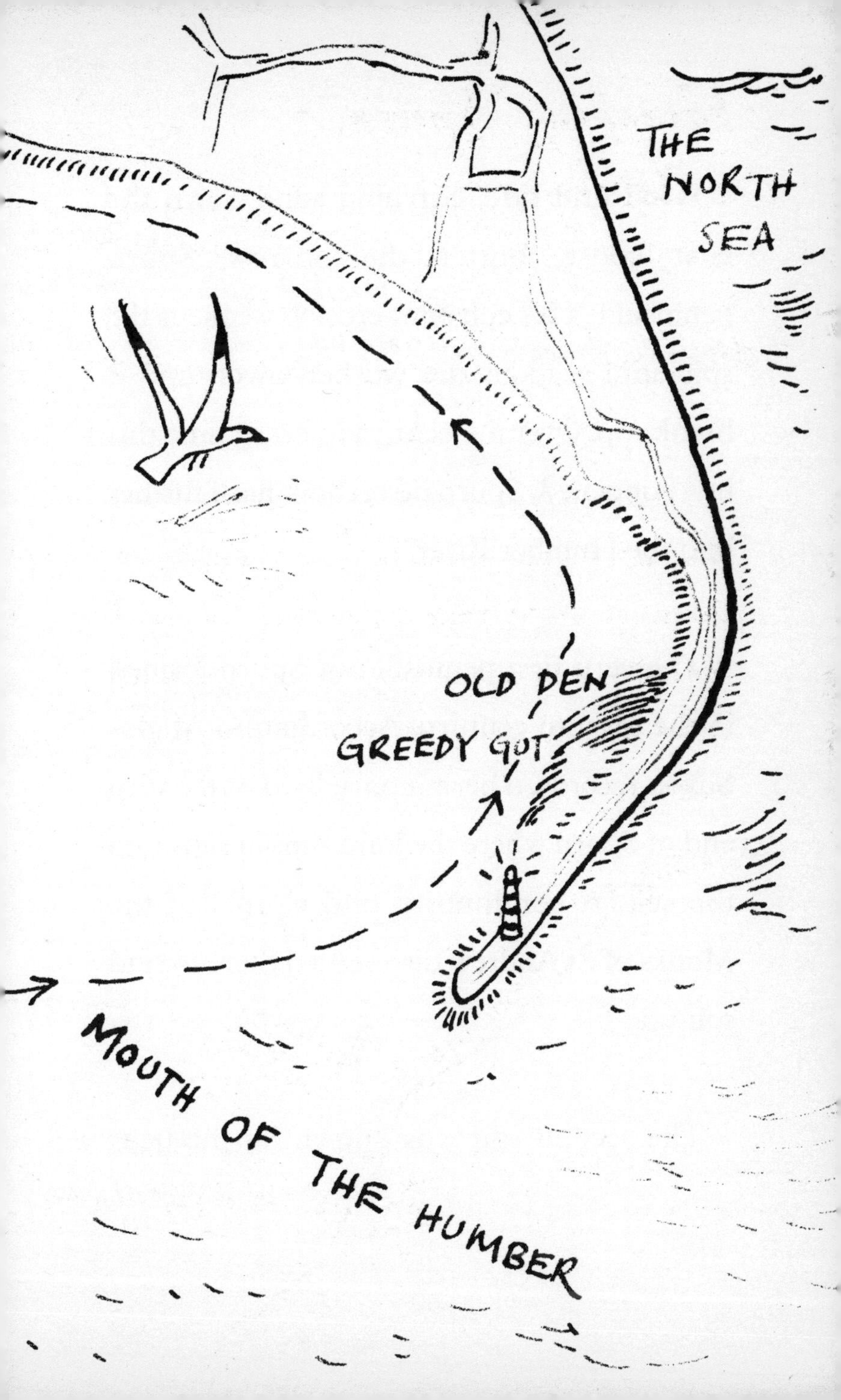
THE NORTH SEA
OLD DEN
GREEDY GUT
MOUTH OF THE HUMBER

Wind and tide, carrying sand down the east coast, batter the narrow Spurn peninsula. This constant erosion weakens the spit until sections are washed away and it breaks up. Over the centuries, every time this has happened, Spurn has rebuilt itself further into the Humber River.

The very first peninsula at Spurn formed in the seventh century. According to Anglo-Saxon records, a hermit once lived at the very end of Spurn where the land simply slips into the sea. A community and chapel of the Monks of St Andrew also settled there to find solitude.

The second spit was known by the year

950, when a Scandinavian called Egil landed on Ravenser, which means 'Raven's sand bank'. The Raven was thought to bring bad luck. It was from Ravenser that the army defeated by Harold at Stamford Bridge sailed in 1066. Harold then marched to Hastings to meet William the Conqueror, where his own good fortune ended.

The third spit was formed when a new sandbank developed in 1230. It was large enough for a town of over three hundred and sixty dwellings. This port was named Ravenser Odd and became a great trading centre, strong enough to rival Grimsby on the far side of the estuary. A number of villages were also built, but vanished some time between 1250 and 1360, overwhelmed by the sea. In 1360, floods and high tides destroyed the remaining communities, including the port. Fishermen say that you can still hear church bells ringing at low tide.

In 1399 Henry IV landed on the fourth spit on his way to take the throne from Richard II. In 1428, a man called Reedbarrow built the first lighthouse to protect shipping approaching the dangerous estuary. This spit flourished during the Wars of the Roses (1455-1487). It was here, in 1471, that Edward IV came ashore from exile on the continent to take England from the ailing Henry VI. Not until 1608 was Spurn yet again destroyed by storms and high seas.

The fifth spit is the isolated peninsula we know today. It is nearly 400 years old, a long time in the history of Spurn. By 1674, this spit was sound enough to build yet another lighthouse, known as Angell's Light. This was replaced by Smeaton's Light in 1776 after a disastrous fire when many people lost their lives.

If you visit Spurn today, and stand at the very end of the narrow spit of land, you can feel the cold wind of a haunted past blowing in your face. It is a desolate, threatening place, the sea washing against your feet, the ships slowly gliding through dazzling sunlight on the immense North Sea. Tens of thousands of migrating waders feed along the mudflats. At any moment, the mudflats may disappear, as the tides thunder against the dunes. Herring gulls wheel and scream, waiting for the sea to decide.

Glossary

aft (page 9)

The stern or rear of a vessel.

estuary (page 12)

The tidal mouth of a large river.

filleting (page 52)

Dividing fish into halves and removing the bones.

foreshore (page 4)

The part of the shore between high and low tide lines.

green water (page 12)

Fishermen commonly refer to deep water as green water.

groyne (page 4)

A wooden breakwater running down the beach to prevent sand drifting. Preserves beaches from erosion by wind and sea.

gunwales (page 7)

The projection above the upper deck level of the sides of a vessel to prevent seawater coming in.

gutting (page 49)

Removing the guts of a fish, the liver to be used for cod-liver oil.

long-line (page 19)

A long fishing line with hooks attached to snoods.

pilot (page 57)

A qualified seaman who knows the local conditions and guides large ships into port.

port (page 9)

The left-hand side of the vessel seen from aft.

skipper (page 12)

Master of any vessel.

snoods (page 28)

Shorter lines attached to the long-line every few yards; the hooks are attached to the snoods.

spit (page 12)

A small point of land running into the sea.

starboard (page 9)

The right-hand side of a vessel seen from aft.

stern (page 6)

The rear of a vessel.

wake (page 58)

The smooth-looking trail of water behind a moving boat.